For Ralf and Greta

Inspired by the short story "The Fir Tree"
by Hans Christian Andersen, first published 1844

First US edition 2021
First published by Templar Books,
an imprint of Bonnier Books UK, 2020

Library of Congress Catalog Card Number pending
ISBN 978-1-5362-2002-5

21 22 23 24 25 26 TLF 10 9 8 7 6 5 4 3 2 1

Printed in Dongguan, Guangdong, China

This book was typeset in Yanar and Diehl Deco.
The illustrations were done in graphite pencil and colored digitally.

TEMPLAR BOOKS
an imprint of
Candlewick Press
99 Dover Street
Somerville, Massachusetts 02144

www.candlewick.com

THE ROBIN &
THE FIR TREE

JASON JAMESON

templar books
an imprint of Candlewick Press

ong ago, in the North, there stood a forest.
The trees of the forest grew tall and old, and many
animals made their homes in and beneath them.

ne day, a tiny robin flew high above the forest, carefully carrying three velvet-red roses. She glided through the clear sky and disappeared among the trees.

In the center of a clearing, a young fir tree woke up. He yawned, stretched, and shook off his cobweb-lace pajamas. "What a beautiful morning it is!" he declared.

Just then, he saw something fluttering in the blue sky above him.

It was the robin. She swooped through his branches, scattering his needles. Finally, she came to rest on a branch, where she carefully placed the roses. The fir tree smiled.

"Thank you, my little friend," the fir tree said. "What a beautiful gift! Where did you get such lovely things?"

rom a garden on the edge of the forest, in a glass house with dancing rainbows inside," the robin chirped.

"I wish I could see such a place," the fir tree said with a sigh. "I only ever see the green of the clearing and the tiny white flowers that grow here."

The next day, the fir tree woke and found the roses withered in the morning sun. Above him, an arrow of geese flew south for the winter. The fir tree wished he could join them and see what they saw.

It was autumn. Many of the trees in the forest had already changed into their gold and orange cloaks, but not the fir tree; he was greener than ever. "Every season will be just the same," he said. "How I long for something different to happen!"

he next day, he got his wish. People arrived in a meadow beside the forest and started building strange wooden structures. All the creatures in the forest chatted about the new arrivals, but the most interested of all was the fir tree.

He strained and stretched to peek past the forest's edge, where he saw towers and a wheel being built. He turned to the robin, who often rested on his branches now, and asked, "What are those wooden things? Have you seen anything like them before?"

The robin nervously ate a small berry— new things always made her nervous.

"People make all kinds of things from trees," she explained, "instruments for music, masts for ships. This thing is called a fair. I've only seen them from high above before."

The fir tree watched until it was dark.

Suddenly, a flash of light shot through the night sky. A thousand colors glittered on the horizon.

The fir tree gasped. "Wake up, little robin!" The robin blinked at the spectacle.

"I wish I could go to the fair myself," said the fir tree. "But my roots hold me here." He rustled his needles gloomily.

The robin fluttered into the air. She didn't like to see her friend sad.

"I have an idea," she announced, and flew into the darkness.

t the forest's edge, there was bonfire smoke and people jostling from one ride to the next. The robin flew above the crowds until she saw a large oak tree, where she stopped to catch her breath.

The fair looked even more beautiful up close, and the robin heard wonderful music, but she also heard the bang and snap of the fireworks, which was very frightening. She wanted to fly back to the fir tree as quickly as she could, but how could she return empty-handed?

Golden ribbons were tied to the oak tree's branches. *These would look wonderful on my friend,* she thought. She picked one up in her beak and darted away from all the noise.

The fir tree sighed with relief when the robin returned. He watched her circle the clearing twice as she wrapped a shimmering gold streamer around him. "This is a ribbon from the fair," she said.

The fir tree puffed up his branches. "How it gleams! It must be wonderful down there." The robin hopped around, delighted that he was happy. She didn't say anything about the scary noises.

"I've asked some friends to help show you what it was like," she twittered. A hundred little fireflies flew around the fir tree, twinkling. "Everything is covered in tiny lights," chirped the robin, "and all the stalls and caravans are splendid colors." Small animals appeared from the undergrowth and made patterns in the fir tree's bark from berries, mushrooms, and flowers. The robin sang her friend a new song that she'd heard on a carousel.

He fell asleep content.

Rain and wind woke the fir tree the next morning. His decorations lay sodden and tattered around him.

The robin flew back to the fairground to find another ribbon, but the fair was gone and everything left behind was torn and broken. When she told the fir tree, his branches drooped sadly.

he orange autumn drained into gray winter. The fir tree slumbered through the cold weeks, not noticing that the world had become glittering and white.

Instead he dreamed he was a tall ship's mast. He would sail through the oceans, leaving the cold seas of the North and venturing to the hot waters and tropical islands of the South. He saw the whole world and he felt free!

One dark afternoon, two men entered the fir tree's clearing. He opened his eyes. Perhaps they had come to take him on an adventure! He watched as they began shaking the surrounding trees, testing them.

Looking over to the fir tree, the men nodded.

As they approached, the robin saw that they carried axes. She froze in fear and whispered, "Don't move—they've seen us." But the fir tree puffed out his branches, straightened his trunk, and made his needles glow the brightest green.

"I have been chosen. It's time to leave," he told her.

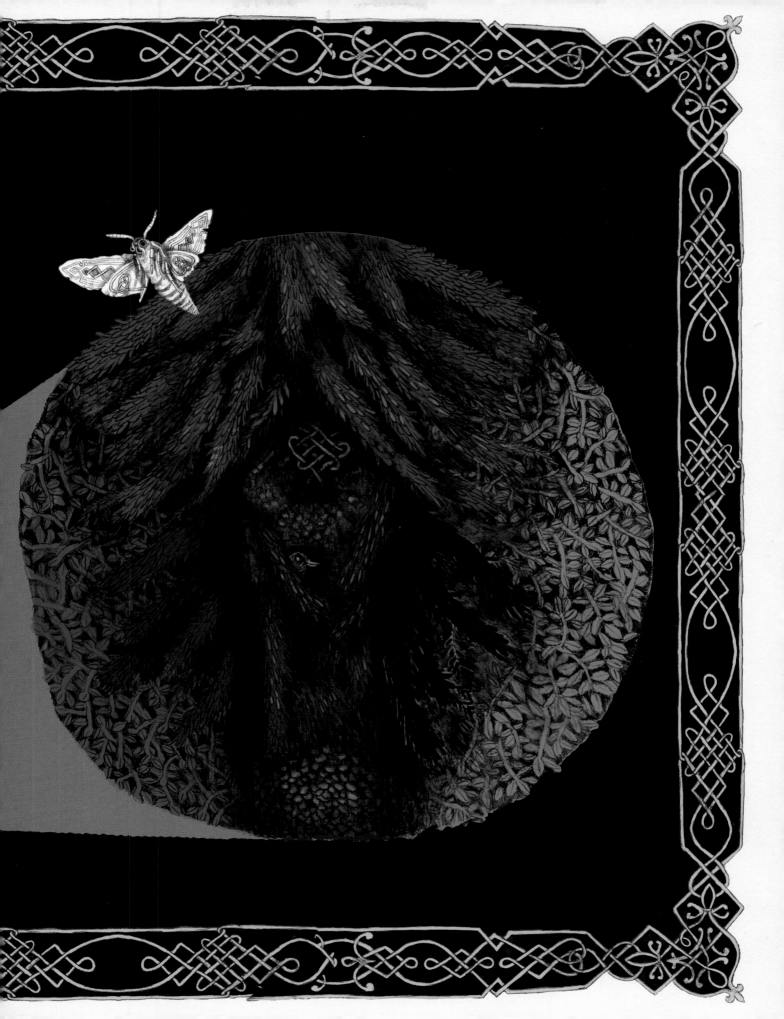

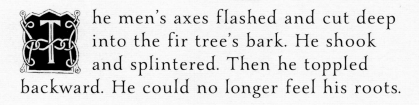he men's axes flashed and cut deep into the fir tree's bark. He shook and splintered. Then he toppled backward. He could no longer feel his roots.

"Goodbye, friend," he said to the robin.

he robin could do nothing to help. She watched the men drag their prize into a van.

The van pulled out of the forest onto a big road, and the robin followed.

Soon she saw the lights of a large town twinkling ahead.

From a chilly window ledge, the little robin looked onto the town square. In the center was a tall structure covered with a tarp. Children and their parents had gathered around it.

Under the tarp, the fir tree could hardly contain his excitement. "They are all here to see me!" he exclaimed.

A t last, the tarp was pulled away. The robin gasped. Her friend looked beautiful. All up and down his branches, glass baubles gleamed and lights sparkled. In a pile around his feet were gold-wrapped presents, and perched on top of his tallest branch was a glowing star.

The fir tree gazed upon the cheering faces of the townspeople.

His voice shaking, he announced, "I am no longer an ordinary tree—I am a beautiful Christmas tree!"

He wasn't sure if they heard him. Children ran at him to tear the gifts from under his branches.

The fir tree spun around, spreading decorations and treats to the onlookers.

"This is wonderful! Take it all!" he shouted.

The robin hopped to a lamppost so she could see better. Close up, the fir tree's glitter and lights looked garish. The children were not gentle, either. They roughly snatched baubles and treats from his limbs.

In a few minutes, branches and trampled needles lay scattered all over the ground. The robin tried to fly to her friend, but some children had started a snowball fight and she was nearly hit. She flew away and hid in a holly tree near the town.

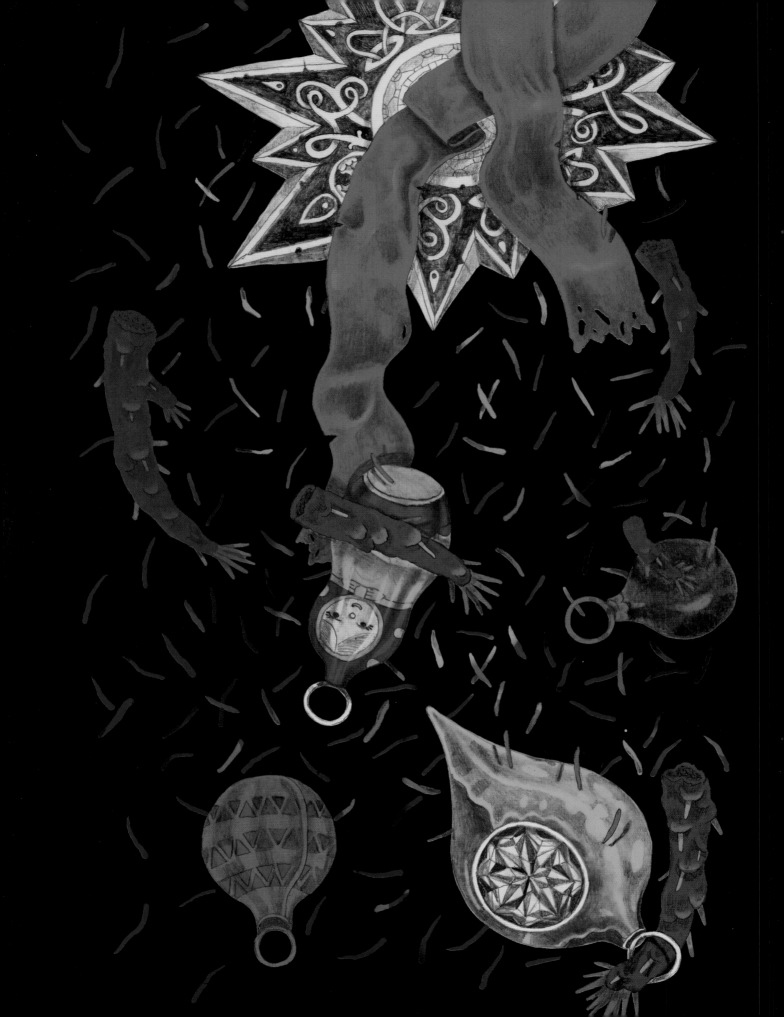

efore long, the fir tree was exhausted. Every twig ached, and his remaining decorations hung heavily, like stones. That night, bright lights and loud bangs spread out above the town.

They were just like the fireworks he'd seen far away at the fair, but up close they were too loud and he worried that a spark might set him on fire.

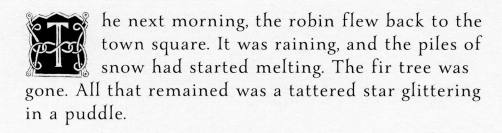

he next morning, the robin flew back to the town square. It was raining, and the piles of snow had started melting. The fir tree was gone. All that remained was a tattered star glittering in a puddle.

She flew down and picked up the star. Her friend would want it back! She began to search for him, but he was nowhere to be found. As the winter days passed, she stayed in town, hoping to see him again.

In a dark corner of the square, rain ran down the rotting roof of an old woodshed and seeped through its walls.

Early that morning, the men who had cut the fir tree down had appeared again. They'd stripped him of the last of his finery, tied ropes around him, and dragged him to the shed.

All he could do was wait and daydream.

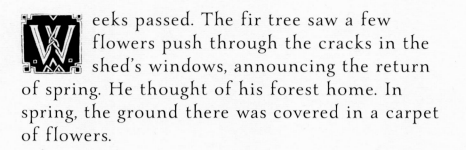

eeks passed. The fir tree saw a few flowers push through the cracks in the shed's windows, announcing the return of spring. He thought of his forest home. In spring, the ground there was covered in a carpet of flowers.

Rustling and scratching from the shadows drew the fir tree's attention to two curious mice. They clambered up his branches and gnawed through a rope, releasing one of his bent limbs. He stretched, cracking his dried branches.

"Oh, how nice it is to be free again," the fir tree said. "Thank you, my little rescuers." He cradled them and one mouse squeaked, "Where are you from and how did you come to be here?"

he fir tree described a beautiful forest clearing, where he was decorated with flowers and fruits.

The mice listened intently, amazed by his story and the many creatures in the wild forest he spoke of.

Just then, there was a noise from outside.

Tap, tap, tap, tap.

The mice scurried across the floor and disappeared.

Who was it?

The fir tree listened for the sound again.

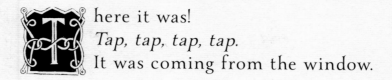 here it was!
Tap, tap, tap, tap.
It was coming from the window.

Through the grimy glass, the fir tree saw his old friend the robin. She hopped through the broken pane.

He shook with amazement. She'd returned! The robin and the fir tree embraced.

"I thought I would never find you," she chirped. She started clearing away dead twigs and brown needles. "What a mess you are."

The fir tree smiled. "I am happy to see you one final time."

harp noises approached the shed. The robin fluttered in a panic. "What do you mean by 'final'?"

The fir tree stroked the robin's feathers. With great effort, he picked off one of his small fir cones and gave it to her. "This is yours. Now fly away—don't stop until you reach the forest. And never come back."

The shed door opened. A man entered. The robin darted past his head, and he tumbled onto the hard floor.

The robin flew high into the twilight. Swooping over the town square, she looked back one last time and saw the man drag the fir tree outside. Seconds later, a dark column of smoke rose above the shed roof, spreading glowing embers through the sky.

ater that night, in the forest clearing, all was quiet. The robin landed on the stump where the fir tree once stood.

She flew to the ground and carefully placed the fir cone in a nest of earth and leaves.

Then she disappeared into the night.

ot so long ago, in the North, there stood a forest. The trees of the forest grew tall and old, and many animals made their homes in and beneath them.

In the center of a clearing, a young fir tree woke up. He yawned and shook off his cobweb-lace pajamas.

Through the gap in the treetops above him, he saw something fluttering toward him. It was a robin. She hopped between his branches, carrying a juicy worm in her beak.

he young fir tree delicately
moved his branches aside
to reveal the robin's nest.
Inside huddled three tiny chicks
and a proud father robin, who
rustled his feathers and hopped
from branch to branch.

omething small caught the glint of the warm spring sun. At the very top of the young fir tree, shining as brightly as ever, was a tattered golden star.